Grim Fairy Tales for Adults

By Steve Brown.

Not all stories have happy endings...

List of Contents

Repugnant
Handful and Glutton
Cider Ella
Little Rude Riding Hood
Tom Thump!
The Elves and the Shed Maker
Doctor White and the Sickly Dwarves
Rumpled Stoats' Skin
The Hare and the Cunning Tortoise
Snoring Beauty
The Slimy Prince
The Pie Maker of Hamelin
The Three Billy Goats Guff
Babes with the Hood
Goldie Strops and the Three Bears
Pus in Boots
The Three Lordly Pigs
Aladdin and the Tragic Lump
Punoakio
Mack and the Bairn Stork.

Repugnant

*Based on **Rapunzel**, a German fairy tale recorded by the Brothers Grimm, and published in 1812.*

Once there lived a handsome Prince,
a carefree bachelor by choice.
One day while riding on his horse,
he heard a distant singing voice.
He scrambled through a tangled wood;
A mighty tower rose aloft.
The voice was coming from above,
a perfect tone so pure and soft.

The tower had no outer door,
but just a window in its turret.
Crumpled men lay round its base;
Did these poor men climb and plummet?
The singing stopped, he heard a sound.
He hid behind some nearby boulders.
A hunched old lady then appeared,
carrying sacks upon her shoulders.

The lady reached the tower and called;
"Rapunzel please let down your hair!"
Then from the window up above,
a sight that made the young prince stare!
A braid of golden hair was lowered,
falling to the ground below.
The lady grabbed onto the hair,
and she was pulled up, moving slow.

She disappeared into the window
with the trail of golden hair.
Did this this lady keep a lonely
secret maiden locked up there?
The Prince returned the following night.
He called up to the room above.
"Rapunzel please let down your hair
I bring my unrequited love."

The hair was lowered, and he climbed.
It was hair-raising, hard and grim.
He slumped inside and saw a short girl
standing with her back to him.
"Please take a seat", the kind girl said
"And have a drink, the climb was steep."
He did so, but he soon felt faint,
and fell into a groggy sleep.

He woke to see a hideous sight.
An ugly slobbering nightmare face!
A cross-eyed girl with hairy warts,
and yellow teeth all out of place!
"I am Repugnant", said the girl.
"And this old lady is my mother.
I've been here for 30 years.
And now my dear you're my next lover!"

"When I've spent my wicked ways,
you'll join the other men I've had.
At the bottom of the tower,
rotting, rank and smelling bad!"
Was this the same girl he'd heard singing?
Words could not describe his shock.
What she lucklessly lacked in looks,
she made up with her lush long locks!

Things were turning ugly now.
No one near would hear him shout.
He focussed on a hair-brained plan,
for there was only one way out.
The Prince he grabbed her trail of hair,
and with a final desperate bound.
He leapt out through the open window,
dropping swiftly to the ground.

Repugnant nosedived close behind,
screaming with her final breath.
The Prince became a monk for life;
The cruel mother starved to death!
But when the new monk prayed at night,
and closed his eyes he saw always.
The hideous, slobbering, gruesome image
of Repugnant's nightmare face!

Handful and Glutton

*Based on **Hansel and Gretel**, a German fairy tale recorded by the Brothers Grimm, and published in 1812.*

Once upon a time there lived
a Farmer and his buxom wife.
He'd tend his cows and sheep all day;
The family lived a simple life.
They had a son whose name was Hans,
but Handful was his cruel nickname.
He was obese and overweight,
and too much eating was to blame.

They also had a daughter Greten;
Everybody called her Glutton.
She was just as big as Hans,
from eating too much beef and mutton.
One day their parents told the pair
to start an exercise regime.
"You need to shift that weight", they said,
"So take a long brisk walk upstream."

"But stay together and keep safe,
because we've heard about a spate.
Of children going missing and
we don't wish you that same sad fate."
After several tiring miles,
the children came across a clearing.
There, they saw an awesome sight,
delicious looking and endearing!

A cottage made of sweets and cakes;
Its roof was lined with wafer tiles.
With window shutters built from buns;
The bricks were fruit cakes stacked in piles!
Lollipops all shaped like flowers.
A Gingerbread and icing door.
Bushes made of candyfloss,
with sweets and chocolates on the floor!

The children started gorging now.
They could not stop, it was sublime.
They munched and ate, 'til bursting full.
They lost all track of any time.
And then a lady old and sweet,
peered out behind the cottage door.
*"What little pretties I have found
eating candy off my floor."*

But then she saw the size of them!
Her cunning plan was sadly foiled.
This Witch had planned to capture them
and in a pot, they would be boiled!
She peered inside her living room;
A child-sized cage was sitting there.
She realised that her iron pot
was far too small to cook this pair!

"Go home my lovelies", said the witch.
"You've had your fill of cakes and sweets."
"No chance", the children both replied.
Then, fully gorged they fell asleep.
The next day when the Witch awoke,
her roof had almost disappeared.
The door and three walls had been scoffed,
just as the wicked Witch had feared.

"You'll eat me out of house and home!"
The Witch screamed, *"This is all I've got!
You'll pay for this!"* and then she started
brewing potions in her pot.
The Farmer and his wife arrived,
from several hours on the road.
They found the ruined eaten house
and two enormous, bloated toads!

The parents took the huge toads home
and placed them in a pond nearby.
And there they spent their last few years,
eating healthy bugs and flies!

Cider Ella

*Based on **Cinderella**, an ancient Greek story recorded by the Brothers Grimm and published in 1812.*

Once there lived a girl called Ella,
in a small house by the sea.
With her mother and her father;
Such a gracious family.
Her father was a Merchant Seaman,
and his hard work bought success.
They moved into a country mansion,
Where they found contentedness.

But fate it dealt a bitter blow,
as some months after they arrived,
Ella's mother caught an illness
and she very sadly died.
After several years alone,
the father found another wife.
He brought her home with her two daughters,
hoping for a fuller life.

The sisters were so plain and ugly,
and they treated Ella bad.
They both were mean and very spiteful,
leaving Ella feeling sad.
The sisters and the cruel stepmother
hated Ella jealously.
Then her father sailed abroad,
and tragically was lost at sea.

Ella turned to drinking cider
trying to drown her troubled grief.
On her 16th birthday Ella,
left the home to walk the streets.
There she ended up a drunkard,
living as a gutter dweller.
Begging folk to buy her drink,
and known to all as Cider Ella!

One day a Royal Page arrived
delivering invites to a Ball.
He noticed Ella by the house
and asked if she lived there at all.
"I did", she muttered drunkenly.
"Well then", he said *"Please do attend.*
Prince Duncan has a Palace Ball,
a Masquerade held next weekend!"

"Every lone girl's been invited
so the Prince may choose a bride".
But Ella knew she could not go.
"I'm such a drunken wretch", she cried.
The big day came, the sisters left,
hoping for the Princes' marriage.
They jeered at Ella as they passed
riding in their budget carriage.

A Fairy God Mum then appeared
and said *"I've watched you all these years.*
It's time I turned your life around.
No more sorrow, pain or tears."
She waved a magic wand and Ella
turned into a fine Princess.
With golden hair, a diamond mask,
glass slippers and a long blue dress!

She made a gilded carriage from
some empty jars of Ella's cider.
Rats became four horses and
a crow became the carriage driver.
Ella now was Ella-gance,
and danced away the magic night.
And when she caught the Prince's eye
he loved her deeply at first sight.

But midnight came, the spell wore off.
She felt again a drunken fool.
She staggered home but, in her rush,
she left a slipper at the ball!
The Prince he searched and finally found
his Ella as a low outcast,
drinking from the matching slipper.
He had found his love at last!

The Fairy God Mum saw the Prince.
"I will grant one wish", she says.
The Prince replied," ***I wish to be
With Ella 'til our dying days."***
Duncan now became Prince Drunken,
in the gutter so carefree.
With his new wife Cider Ella,
where they drank so merrily!

Little Rude Riding Hood

*Based on **Little Red Riding Hood**, a European fairy tale recorded by the Brothers Grimm and published in 1812.*

Once there lived a headstrong girl
besides the outskirts of a wood.
Because she was a spoilt young brat,
her nickname was Rude Riding Hood.
She always wore a hooded coat,
crimson red and buttoned tight.
The villagers they kept their distance,
and avoided her on sight.

One day she told her mother, *"I am
off to see poor Grandma now."*
Make me up some food to take;
She's bound to want some, greedy cow!"
Her mother packed a box of food,
and warned her not to talk to strangers.
"Go straight to her house my dear;
The woods can sometimes harbour dangers.

A wolf was spotted just last month",
but then Rude Riding Hood replied;
"Oh, stupid mother, do not fuss
I'll go straight there, I wouldn't lie."
Halfway through the dense dark wood,
she felt quite peckish, so she sat,
and scoffed the food her mother packed.
"It'll only make poor Grandma fat!"

Just then a Woodsman wandered by.
He carried an enormous axe.
"You shouldn't be alone he said.
I'll shield you if a wolf attacks!"
"You'd be useless", she replied
"You really wouldn't have a clue!"
I must not talk to any stranger,
and there's none stranger than you!"

"How rude", the shocked young Woodsman thought.
"And what a dreadful way to talk."
He stomped away and let the brat
continue on her woodland walk.
She reached her Grandma's lonely house;
The night was slowly drawing in.
She banged upon its wooden door;
There was no answer from within.

She shouted through the letterbox;
"Hey open up you lazy mare!"
Grandma's crackly voice replied;
"Who's loudly shouting from out there?"
"Your sweet grandchild", said the girl.
"I'm coming in I've had enough."
She barged in as her Grandma moaned;
"I'm sorry dear I'm feeling rough."

In a corner dark and dim,
her Grandma lay upon her bed.
A blanket pulled up to her neck.
A shawl was wrapped around her head.
"What's the matter", asked the child;
"Your voice sounds strangely different now."
"I have a fever", Grandma said,
and wiped a cloth across her brow.

"You won't get sympathy from me!"
the rude child said, *"And what are those?"*
She pointed to her Grandma's ears;
"They're big and hairy like your nose!"
"And what big eyes you have Grandma!
Open wide and bloodshot red."
"All the better to see the full moon,
through my window", Grandma said.

"And what big teeth you have Grandma!
Do you still soak them overnight?"
"All the better to bite you with,
you little upstart! Grandma cried.
Her Grandma suddenly transformed;
A snarling werewolf bit the child.
The girl let out a hideous scream.
The Woodsman nearby, simply smiled.

The child was never heard again,
but several folk have often said.
They've seen two wolves, and one of them,
has long red fur upon its head!

Tom Thump!

*Based on **Tom Thumb**, an English Folklore fairy tale first published in 1621.*

In a sleepy country village,
lived a Tailor with his wife.
They had tried, but failed to have
children all their married life.
One day the wife she knelt and prayed;
"Oh, please give me a little boy.
One who has a great big heart,
and one who'll bring us years of joy?"

Her wish was granted and that year,
she gave birth to a tiny son.
But sadly, as she held her child,
she saw a sight that left her numb.
The boy possessed a huge right fist,
five times bigger than the other.
She gave a scream and at that point,
the baby punched his distraught mother!

She looked down at her smiling boy
and said, *"I should be grateful though.*
You're strong and healthy, I will call
you Tom and we will cope somehow."
She hid away for several months,
then held a christening at the church.
The vicar held the baby Tom,
then *"THUMP!"* He gave a backward lurch.

The vicar staggered back in shock;
"I name this strong child Thomas Thump!"
He swiftly handed back the child,
and nursed a glowing big red lump.
Five years passed and Tom he grew,
but by the time he started school.
His right fist had become immense,
whilst Tom was only two foot tall!

One day a teacher bought Tom home.
Six boys had teased him being small.
"He's been quite heavy handed, and
the six boys are in hospital!"
On his return Tom earned respect.
He overcame his many hurdles.
Wrestling bouts he won hands down,
but swimming left him turning circles!

One spring, a travelling fair arrived
with sideshows and a wooden stage.
It held an open competition,
for fist fighting in a cage.
Tom, he entered. What a star!
He beat all-comers with such ease.
He'd thump them in the midriff and
then finish them upon their knees!

"Please give Tom a great big hand!"
The owner cried, then said to Tom;
"You'll make a fistful for us both,
let's tour the country, come along!"
So, Tom left school and made his fortune
beating everyone in sight.
He even rid a village of a Giant
with his powerful right!

Tom returned a rich young man
and bought his parents a new home.
He took a quiet job digging graves
in the churchyard all alone.
On Palm Sunday he heard screams;
A fire was raging in the church!
The villagers were trapped inside;
He ran and gave the door a lurch.

The church was full of thick black smoke,
but being little, Tom he found,
that he could see unconscious bodies
lying nearby on the ground.
He dragged them out, three at a time,
into the open air outside.
He ran in time and time again,
but sadly on his last run died.

In time the church was renovated,
Toms' mum used his fortune won.
They named the church St. Thomas's
in tribute to their fallen son.
A statue was erected outside.
On a plaque was written down.

"In memory of our hero Tom,
who single-handedly saved the town!"

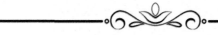

The Elves and the Shed Maker

*Based on **The Elves and the Shoemaker**, a German fairy tale recorded by the Brothers Grimm and published in 1812.*

In a quiet peaceful village
lived a Carpenter by trade.
He made a modest income from
the simple furniture he made.
Using timber from the woods,
he crafted tables, chairs, and beds.
But little did he realise that
he'd make his fortune building sheds!

One day with his retirement near,
his wife suggested that he should
build a modest garden shed
from his old left-over wood.
And so, he gathered up the piles
and laid them on his workshop floor.
He drew rough plans to build this shed,
then feeling tired he locked the door.

"I'm getting too old for this work".
he said, *"I need an easy life.*
I wish that I could settle down
and spend time with my darling wife."
A new day dawned; the old man dressed,
and trudged on down the path that led
to his workshop by the woods,
to build his small retirement shed.

He opened up his workshop door
and stood astounded at the sight!
A stunning ornate wooden shed
had been constructed overnight!
The craftsmanship was just superb,
with leaf shaped carvings round the door,
and lattice edging on the roof,
with raised tree motifs on the floor.

He asked some local friends to move
the shed onto his lawn outside.
The villagers were so impressed
they ordered sheds to be supplied.
And so, each day he'd gather wood
and lay it on the workshop floor.
And each dawn as a shed appeared
his curiousness grew more and more.

And so, one night he hid inside
his workshop cupboard out of sight.
And soon he heard soft steps approach,
and saw his oil lamp come alight.
Ten enchanting two-foot Elves
had climbed in through some broken vents.
The Elves collected up his tools
and set to work with diligence.

They toiled all night then bang on **shed**-ule,
finished at the light of day.
They tidied up and swept the floor,
then disappeared upon their way.
The carpenter was overwhelmed
and sought a way to thank these Elves.
He drew up plans for ten tree houses
that the Elves could build themselves.

That night he hid expectantly
and watched the eager Elves prepare.
And then they stopped and stared in awe
upon the new plans lying there.
They danced and skipped excitedly,
then built their houses with delight.
They dragged them through the broken vents
and disappeared into the night.

The Carpenter lived ten more years,
a happy, rich contented life.
But then one day he fell quite ill
and called to his beloved wife.
*"Please place these plans inside my shop
and leave the oil lamp burning bright."*
And so, she did, but sadly then
her husband died that very night.

Next day she found an ornate coffin
beautifully covered in veneer.
Ten elves stood sadly with heads bowed,
and all of them they **shed** a tear...

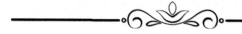

Doctor White and the Sickly Dwarfs

*Based on **Snow White**, a German fairy tale recorded by the Brothers Grimm and published in 1812.*

Disclaimer: Due to copyright laws, the Dwarfs names portrayed in this story have been changed to protect their real identity!

$\mathfrak{I}$n a Palace lived a young girl,
Princess Florence was her name.
With long black curls and pale white skin,
her looks put other girls to shame.
Her cruel Stepmum held the throne;
She treated Flo White with contempt.
The girl became her Palace slave,
dishevelled dirty and unkempt.

To pass the boredom Flo would climb
the Palace tower every day.
The Household Doctor and Physician
lived there quietly, old and grey.
They proved good friends and Flo she watched him
making potions for the sick.
She studied hard and learnt his craft,
and picked up useful treatments quick.

One day a messenger arrived
for the Doctor's healing skill.
A Dwarf residing by the forest
had become extremely ill.
"I'm way too old to travel far."
said the Doctor, *"But I know.*
That Doctor White is more than able.
Take my bag, and quickly go!"

And so, she travelled through the forest
to a cottage by a lake.
She knocked the door then heard a voice
say; *"Go away for goodness sake!"*
"It's the Doctor", Flo replied,
"and who is keen for me to go?"
The door was opened by a dwarf;
"I'm GROUCHY if you need to know!"

The Dwarfs they introduced themselves.
The sight of Flo had made them glad.
They took her to a bed upstairs;
"So this is DOK he's feeling bad.
He usually takes good care of us,
but recently he's lost the will.
We've all got problems of our own;
They're making him feel very ill."

"Very well," Flo White replied.
"I'll look at each of you in turn.
I'll start with GROUCHY; you're short tempered,
decent manners you must learn.
Here are tablets for depression;
They will level up your moods.
DROWSY, here's some vitamin pills,
no more junk or fatty foods.

DIPPY, you need quick brain training.
Here's a book to boost your mind.
TIMID, you need confidence classes;
I'll sign you up if you're inclined.
SNIFFY, stay away from pollen.
Here's some Antihistamine.
And MERRY, alcohols your problem.
Ditch the drink until you're clean."

Back at home Flo's blonde Stepmother
stood and stared upon a wall.
"Mirror, mirror on the wall
who's the fairest of them all?"
"You are, Queen," the mirror said,
"as Flo white's hair is black of course!"
"Where's she now?" the mad Queen raged.
"She's at the cottage of the Dwarfs."

Flo, she stayed there overnight,
and DOK seemed better by the dawn.
They gave Flo White a big red apple
for her journey travelling home.
It was a gift a fair old lady
handed in that very day!
You know the phrase, an apple of death
keeps the Doctor well away!

Rumpled Stoat's Skin

*Based on **Rumpelstiltskin**, a German fairy tale recorded by the
Brothers Grimm and published in 1812.*

$\mathfrak{I}$n a kingdom far away
lived a Miller, meek and poor.
One day the old King sent his men
collecting taxes at his door.
The Miller said *"I cannot pay you;*
I am penniless and old.
But you can take my daughter here,
for she can spin straw into gold!"

The men were doubtful, but they took
the daughter off to see the King.
The King was also sceptical
and locked her in his castle wing.
"I'll give you one whole week to spin
some gold from all these bales of straw.
But if you can't your fathers' Mill
will then belong to him no more!"

The daughter cried for several days
and would not touch the spinning wheel.
But when the seventh day arrived,
she prayed to have the magic skill.
And then a funny Imp appeared.
He wore a wrinkled coat of fur.
He said that he could spin the straw
and turn it into gold for her!

But first she must provide a gift.
"I have this necklace", she replied.
It was my mothers' treasured piece
before she very sadly died."
And so, the curious Imp sat down
and breathed onto the spinning wheel.
And then he spun long threads of gold,
and soon the room began to fill.

When sunrise came, the King appeared
and stood there awestruck at the sight.
Baskets full of golden thread,
glimmering and glistening bright!
The sight of so much golden thread
then made the king a greedy man.
He bought in twice as many bales
than the first batch she had spun.

"You must remain another week
to spin more gold from all this straw.
And in return your father's debts
will be forgotten ever more."
And so, the Imp appeared again.
This time she gave the Imp a ring.
A present from her father,
she had handed over everything!

The King was so ecstatic that
he took a pity on the girl.
"One more week of spinning gold,
your father will become an Earl.
And you shall have your freedom girl,
together with a chest of gold.
And I shall make you up a member
of my royal King's household."

The Imp appeared again that week
and saw the daughter so distraught.
"I haven't any gifts" she said,
in return for your support."
"Then give me up your first-born child
or else you'll never be set free."
And so, he spun for one last time,
as she agreed reluctantly.

Several happy years passed by;
She lived a life of luxury.
But when her first born child arrived,
the Imp appeared quite suddenly.
She offered him her worldly wealth,
yet all he wanted was her child.
"But I will give you one last chance,"
he said, and then he wryly smiled.

"I'll give you five attempts to guess
my real name by tomorrow night.
But if you can't, the child is mine."
And then he turned and took his flight.
She swiftly followed in his wake
and saw him sneak into a wood.
And then she heard him singing softly
by a campfire where he stood.

"Tomorrow night new plans I make.
The riddle she will never crack it.
Her baby I will surely take.
My name is taken from my jacket!"
The following night the Imp returned.
The girl she stared at what he wore.
"Is it Pleated Polecat Pelt?
Or even Wrinkled Weasel Fur?"

"No" he told her, sounding worried,
"You will have to guess again."
"Have you Crumpled Ferret Fleece
or Crinkled Mink Hide for your name?"
The Imp was really sweating now;
He knew that she was getting close.
"Rumpled Stoats Skin is your name!"
The Imp went white and promptly froze.

"No!" he screamed and leapt out of
the window splattering everywhere!
The daughter smiled down at her babe,
and stroked her golden straw-like hair.

The Hare and the Cunning Tortoise

*Based on **The Tortoise and the Hare,** which is one of Aesop's Fables.*

In a small town far away
was a most peculiar sight.
All its folk were animals,
civilised and quite polite.
They ran the town all by themselves,
foxes, badgers, storks and rats.
All had different parts to play,
these Tortoises and hares and cats.

One fine day a crowd assembled.
Mr Tortoise, they were told,
would hold a weekly running race,
the entrance fee was each five gold.
He, and one competitor
would run a two-mile laid out track.
The winner would take all the gold;
It really was as plain as that.

Mr Hare was so excited,
placing down his name to run.
The Tortoise was extremely slow;
The Hare was swift as anyone.
And so, the race was held next day,
officials on the finish line.
Animals were placing bets,
waging on the Hare this time.

And off they raced, the Hare so fast,
disappearing out of sight.
The Tortoise he was slow and steady,
plodding on with all his might.
Halfway round, the Hare slowed down
besides a farmer's well stocked field.
He sat and munched upon some carrots,
as he knew the race was sealed.

Feeling energised and fresh,
he carried on at steady pace.
But as he reached the finish straight
he saw that he had lost the race!
The Tortoise had just crossed the line;
They lifted him, the cheering crowds.
That slowcoach he had beaten him,
and won the gold, he knew not how.

The Hare was angry with himself;
He'd been a brash conceited fool.
He challenged for another race,
this time he wouldn't stop at all.
The Tortoise smiled but warned the Hare
the entrance fee was now ten gold.
The Hare had lost his savings so,
his prized possessions must be sold.

The race was held the following week.
The Hare ran off, away he sped.
But when he turned the final bend
he saw the Tortoise up ahead!
He made a Hare-culian sprint.
This was a case of life or death.
But all his efforts were in vain.
The Tortoise won by one Hares breadth!

The Hare he knew that he'd been cheated,
but he couldn't prove a thing.
And so, he waited for a week
when Mr Fox was challenging.
Twenty gold was now the fee.
Mr Fox he picked up pace.
The Hare took shorts cuts through the fields,
watching closely at the race.

At the first bend Mr Tortoise
dived into a nearby wood.
The Hare raced to the finish line
and then he finally understood.
A tortoise walked out of the woods
on the last bend of the road.
And then across the finish line
the Tortoise confidently strode.

And now he knew the cunning ploy.
The Tortoise had a secret twin!
The Hare would have to sell his house
if he was ever going to win.
He challenged for a final race:
Forty gold he had to pay!
He paid the Fox to grab the twin
before the race was underway.
And so, the final race began.
The hare raced off at breakneck speed.
And on the final bend he saw
the twin tied up against a tree!
But then he saw the finish straight.
He stared in utter disbelief.
The Tortoise had just crossed the line;
The Hare collapsed upon his knees.

The Fox was led away and charged
with kidnap, threatening and assault.
The Hare was homeless, and forlorn.
This turtle mess was all his fault.
The Tortoise Twins they walked away,
clutching at their winning prize.
They waved up to their helpful ally.
Mr Stork up in the sky!

Snoring Beauty

*Based on **Sleeping Beauty**, a German fairy tale recorded by the Brothers Grimm and published in 1812.*

In a Palace by a river
lived a noble King and Queen.
The couple had a new-born girl
and planned a lavish christening.
All the wealthy were invited
to the chapel in their grounds.
In attendance were Godmothers
in their sparkling sequined gowns.

They were granting baby wishes,
such as happiness and wealth.
Other blessings gave her beauty,
kindness, wisdom, strength and health.
Suddenly there was a flash!
It was an evil Godmother.
She was vexed an invitation
hadn't been dispatched to her!

"I will curse your Annabel
before her sixteenth year arrives.
She'll prick her finger on a needle.
From its poison she will die!"
She vanished, and the King and Queen
were mortified she would not live.
But then the last Godmother said;
"I have a final wish to give."

"The curse is strong, it cannot be
undone but I can calm your fears.
The Princess she will only snooze
for a period of two years."
And then the final wish was cast
with a feeble spluttering.
All spinning wheels were duly banned
from the Palace by the King.

The baby grew into a girl,
a gracious, happy, charming child.
At fifteen she was beautiful.
Her parents they were so beguiled.
The curse had been forgotten now;
Her sixteenth birthday slowly loomed.
Then one dark night, she could not sleep
and so her dreadful fate was doomed.

She wandered through the castle floors
and saw a stairwell leading down.
The stairs were crumbling, cracked and steep;
She climbed down pulling up her gown.
An old oak door was at its base.
A rusty key was in its lock.
She walked into a damp room where,
a woman gave her quite a shock.

She sat beside a spinning wheel,
sobbing underneath her veil,
"Oh, pretty girl, I need your help,
my fingers are so weak and frail."
The Princess went to hold her hands
but pricked her finger on the needle.
She staggered to a grand old bed,
feeling poisoned, weak and feeble.

The Palace woke the following day
to a loud and rumbling sound.
The walls were shaking violently
like an earthquake in the ground.
They found the Princess in the basement,
snoring loudly on the bed.
The King he then recalled the curse
and realised with an awful dread.

She wouldn't snooze for two long years;
She snores and keeps them all awake!
She was nick-named Decibel;
The King made plans for all their sake.
"To any man that swiftly cures
the Princess of this snoring spell.
Her hand in marriage is the prize.
You must act fast, we cannot dwell."

Many men they tried their luck,
putting mint upon her tongue.
Placing pegs upon her nose,
garlic, ginger, onion.
Tying balls upon her back
to make her sleep upon her side.
Filling up the room with steam
and forcing nasal airways wide.

After weeks, a man arrived;
He'd built a very strange device.
A rubber mouthpiece joined up to
a wooden tube, to be precise.
"It's called a "SNORE-KILL", said the man,
and tied the Princess to the bed.
And when he placed it in her mouth
it stopped the deafening snoring dead!

And so, the Palace slept in peace.
They had this clever man to thank.
But one dark night there came a storm;
The nearby river burst its bank.
The basement flooded six-feet-high;
The King rushed in and feared the worst.
But luckily the Snore-kill saved her,
even though she was submersed.

The clever man then built a mask
and rubber flippers like a duck.
And while he waited for his bride,
he ran a scuba diving club!

The Slimy Prince

*Based on **The Frog Prince**, a German fairy tale recorded by the Brothers Grimm and published in 1812.*

$\mathfrak{I}$n a castle, far away
lived a Princess, fair and tall.
She spent her spare time every day
playing with a golden ball.
One day, while juggling with the ball,
it fell into her garden pond.
It disappeared into its depth.
The treasured toy she loved so fond!

As she cried there helplessly,
a frog hopped out and startled her.
"Hello Darlin', why the tears?
Tell me what you're crying for."
She told him of her sunken ball.
The creepy frog said, *"Never mind.*
I'll get your ball out, but you have to
give me favours back in kind."

"I'll give you anything you want!"
wailed the princess through her tears.
And so the slimy frog dived in
and with her ball he reappeared.
The Princess she was overjoyed,
but then the frog reminded her.
"Remember that you promised me
gratuity for its return!"

"I want to be your friend and eat
the same meals as yourself", he said.
And live with you inside the Castle,
sleeping with you in your bed!"
"You've got some balls!" the Princess cried,
but she agreed and ran back home.
She ran up to her bedroom where,
she sobbed for hours all alone.

When morning came, the King he found
the frog outside his Castle door.
The frog then told the startled King
the promises his daughter swore.
The Princess begged her father not
to let the horrid reptile in.
"A promise is a promise dear,
you'll keep your word now", said the King.

At dinner time, a meal arrived
inside some silver serving dishes.
"I have ordered food my dear;
It really will be quite delicious!"
The Princess lifted up the lids
and looked in horror at the food.
Slugs and snails and worms and flies,
piled up high and lightly stewed!

"You will grow to love this food"
said the frog after the meal.
"And now it's time to go to bed.
You promised and a deal's a deal!"
The Princess placed him on her pillow,
this, the worst day of her life.
"Now kiss me on the mouth he said,
and I will take you for my wife!"

"No!" she screamed, and so he told her
of an evil Witches spell
that turned him into this poor frog,
and left him in the pond to dwell.
He used to be a noble Prince,
and would not find true love, unless,
a Princess kissed him on the lips
and brought him lasting happiness.

And so she kissed him tentatively,
and in a flash they fell in love.
She saw his perfect handsome face
staring down at her above.
He had the most impressive warts
and big black eyes she'd ever seen!
And his skin was silky smooth,
shiny wet and mottled green!

And so the two frogs hopped on down
and left the Castle blissfully.
They leapt into the garden pond
and there they lived so hoppily!

The Pie Maker of Hamelin

*Based on **The Pied Piper of Hamelin**, a German fairy tale recorded by the Brothers Grimm and published in 1812.*

Hamelin was a small quaint town
in the heart of Germany.
The townsfolk lived a simple life
filled with peace and harmony.
However, in the last few months
a feline flu wiped out their cats.
And now the town was overrun
by a plague of hungry rats!

The rats were swarming everywhere,
in the shops and through the street.
In the houses inns and schools,
scurrying beneath their feet.
The Town Mayor offered a reward;
Two hundred gold to anyone,
who'd rid the menace of the rats,
before the plague killed everyone.

The news spread fast across the town
to the local village Baker.
He was known to everyone
as the famous Town Pie-Maker.
The Baker went to see the Mayor
and told him of his cunning plan.
He'll bake a hundred meaty pies
just as quickly as he can.

He would lure the hungry rats
to his Bakery and then,
he'd lock them in an empty barn
he used to store his excess grain.
Once inside the rats would starve.
With no escape, it was secure.
His other barn was full of grain,
so he could bake on as before.

"You'll never need to bake again,"
the Mayor said *"With your reward.*
The sooner that we rid this town
of rats, the better for us all."
And so, the Baker baked his pies
and left them in the midday sun.
And soon the smell of putrid meat
could now be by smelled by everyone.

He laid the pies out on the road
and made a long trail to the barn.
And soon the rats were swarming out;
The potent stench had worked its charm!
Hundreds ran into the barn,
and finally they all were snared.
The Baker locked them all inside,
then hurried off to see the Mayor.

The Mayor was overjoyed but said;
"It didn't take you long to do.
For just a day's work, twenty gold
is adequate reward for you!"
The Baker stormed off in a rage.
He hatched a new revengeful plan.
He'd get his full and just reward
off that ungrateful selfish man!

One week later on a Sunday,
all the townsfolk sang and prayed
in the church for evening worship
whilst at home their children laid.
The Baker drove his cart to town
and shouted in the empty streets.
"Come and get delicious pies,
they're free and full of tasty treats!

Strawberries and chocolate flakes,
soft marshmallows full of cream!"
And soon a line of sleepy children
followed wide-eyed in a dream.
By the time they reached his barns
the night was misty black and dark.
He ushered all the children in
and passed them pies upon his cart.

Three days later, all the town
were gathered round the worried Mayor.
The Baker pointed at the Mayor
and said, *"The problem's standing there.*
He needs to now eat humble pie;
He short changed me to trap the rats."
The Mayor paid up, the baker went
to fetch the kidnapped children back.
He opened up the grain barn door
and stared inside with mouth agape.
The barn was only full of grain!
Had all the children since escaped?
And then he realized he had placed
the children in the other barn!
He loudly screamed and with the gold,
he fled the village in alarm.

The barn door started creaking now.
This time the Baker he had blundered.
But as he crossed the village border
there was just one thing he wondered.
Were there giant rats inside?
All with a taste for infant meat?
Or were there rabid children all
with half chewed rats around their feet?

The Three Billy Goats Guff

*Based on **The Three Billy Goats Gruff**, a Norwegian fairy tale first published in 1841.*

Once there lived three billy goats
in a valley lush and green.
A deep stream cut between two fields,
with an arched bridge in between.
The goats had feasted in one field
and now this field was looking bare.
All the turnips sprouts and grass
had been consumed without a care!

Now they looked across the stream
into a green and well stocked field.
They'd have to cross the rickety bridge
to reach this tempting luscious yield.
But underneath this wooden bridge
there hid a very hungry Troll.
He'd love to capture one or more,
and crunch their tasty bodies whole!

First there came the youngest goat;
"Tip Tap, Tip Tap, Tip Tap, Tip!"
"Who's that crossing on my bridge?"
bawled the Troll, *"I'm trying to kip!"*
A tiny nervous voice replied;
"I'm Billy the Kid, I'm on my way.
to reach the next field full of sprouts,
turnips, grass and tasty hay."

"Well, it's time to eat you now!"
roared the Troll, but in his fright,
the kid released a stinking guff
with all his able strength and might!
"Oh that's bad!" exclaimed the Troll,
and fell back coughing violently.
The little goat ran to the field
and started eating hungrily.

Twenty minutes later on,
"Trip trap, trip trap", the planks went.
"Who's that crossing on my bridge
without permission or consent?"
"I'm Billy Ricky", said the goat;
"The other field is now my goal.
I'm off to join my brother there."
"No kidding", said the angry Troll.

"Well it's time to eat you now!"
Exclaimed the Troll, but in his fright,
the bigger goat released a putrid
guff with all his brawn and might.
"Oh good grief!" exclaimed the Troll,
and fell into the stream below.
The Wiley goat had held his breath,
then ran to join his little bro'.

Twenty minutes later on;
"Clip clop, clip clop", went the bridge.
A deep and booming voice proclaimed;
"I'm well aware of where you're hid."
"I am the dreaded Goat-father
I'm not afraid unlike my sons."
And then he let rip one huge guff.
The most humungous ever done!

Up leapt the Troll onto the bridge,
a blanket wrapped around his face!
The goat was startled open mouthed,
and breathed his lethal toxic waste!
Twenty minutes later on,
the noxious cloud had all dispersed.
The Troll he dragged the father home.
His scape-goat sons they feared the worst!

The Troll dragged out his cooking pot
and set the table with his bowl.
He relished eating every day,
this tasty goat meat casserole!

Babes with the Hood

*Based on **Babes in the Wood**, a traditional English children's tale first published in 1595.*

Once there lived a Prince and Princess
in a Castle far away.
The Prince was eight, his sister six,
and life was sweet until one day.
Their parents drowned when out to sea,
and so their care was handed down
to their evil Uncle who, was keen
to claim his Nephew's crown!

The Uncle hatched a gruesome plan
to hire some local ruffian men.
And take the children to the woods,
then cruelly kill and bury them!
And so the babes they left the Castle,
with the men into the woods.
In a clearing, bound and gagged,
the crying frightened children stood.

Suddenly, a shaft of arrows
hurtled through the woodland trees.
The ruffian men died instantly,
the scared young captives they were free!
A man approached them dressed in green;
He knelt in front of where they stood.
"Wassup dudes, your fate is good.
My name is Rappa of da Hood."

The children told him who they were,
and of their evil Uncle's plan.
"You should join my crazy clan
to kill dis disrepectin' man!"
And so the children joined his band
of outlaws, crooks and profiteers.
"Meet my bangin' volunteers
of archers, thieves and racketeers."

"Here's Will Scarface, Li'l John,
Friar Shmuck, Mad Marion.
They will teach you from now on.
No dude will miss you while you're gone."
Years went by: the children grew,
and learned the arts of swordsmanship,
archery and camouflage,
and combat skills and craftsmanship.

One day their Uncle King announced
a tournament of Archery
to celebrate his ten year rule:
The children entered secretly.
Rappa's men they entered too,
forty thieves disguised as Earls.
The Prince he won the young boys match,
the Princess won the match for girls.

The Prince and Princess climbed the stairs
towards their Uncle on his throne.
He was handing out the medals
to the winners on his own.
"Wassup Uncle!" said the Prince.
"Remember us ten years ago?"
The King went white and staggered back.
Forty archers aimed their bows.

Waves of arrows cut the air
all from the bows of Rappa's men.
Their Uncle's troops and bodyguards,
they fell as arrows pummelled them.
The Prince addressed the startled crowd;
"I am your rightful heir and King!
Our Uncle tried to kill us both,
but now we'll redress everything."

The huge crowd cheered and welcomed back
the children rescued by the Hood.
Their Uncle, hoodwinked, bound and gagged
was dragged into the nearby wood.
Rappa's men now known as "Hoodies",
kept the streets secure and safe.
The Prince he ruled for many years,
a prosperous and peaceful place.

Goldie Strops and the Three Bears

*Based on **Goldilocks and the Three Bears**, a British fairy tale first published in 1837.*

In a cottage near some woods
lived a small bear family.
Why they didn't live together
in a normal cave beats me!
On this sunny autumn day
the three bears went out for a bit.
The Papa, Mama, Baby bear,
in the woods to take a short stroll!

Meanwhile up the cottage path
strolled a blonde girl feeling tired.
Known to all as Goldie Strops;
A fussy spoilt conceited child.
She banged the door, with no response.
It was unlocked, the careless fools!
She wandered in, oh what a mess!
The owners lived like animals!

And then she smelled their fresh made porridge
cooling on the kitchen top.
The porridge sat in three sized bowls;
The first big bowl was steaming hot.
"Argh!" she cried, *"I've burnt my tongue!"*
and dropped the bowl upon the floor.
The second bowl was lumpy cold;
She threw it at the kitchen door!

The little bowl was just so right
But then as she began to eat,
she noticed three sized wooden chairs,
and sat down on the largest seat.
"Ooh!" she moaned, *"This seat's too hard!"*
And kicked the chair until it broke!
The medium chair was far too soft;
She ripped its stuffing in a stroke!

The smallest chair was excellent;
She gulped the porridge wanting more.
But this chair couldn't **bear** her weight,
and splintered on the kitchen floor!
And then she suddenly felt tired
and wandered upstairs for a snooze.
She saw three beds inside the room,
but knew this time which one to choose!

In time the three bears wandered home,
and saw an awful **grizzly** sight.
The porridge splattered on the floor,
the broken chairs, who caused this plight?
"Someone's eaten all my porridge!"
Wailed the crying Baby bear.
"What a mess they've made", he sobbed.
"And where's my favourite little chair?"

The Papa flew into a rage,
and rushed upstairs and saw her there.
Sprawled across the Baby's bed,
sleeping soundly, without care!
Goldie Strops had gone too far,
and she was never heard again.
But passers-by believe they've glimpsed
a sad young cleaner clapped in chains!

Pus in Boots

*Based on **Puss in Boots**, an Italian fairy tale first published in 1550.*

Once there lived an old Innkeeper
with his three sons at his Inn.
When the old Innkeeper died,
the first two sons took everything.
The eldest son he took the Inn,
the second all the valuables.
The youngest son was left with just
a cat, some grain and vegetables!

The youngest son was very cross;
"I've nothing but this stupid cat!"
The cat replied: *"I'm not so stupid;*
I can talk and help you out!
Master, give me grain and carrots;
See what wonders I can do!
Lend me please your childhood jacket
and your hat and leather boots."

The son was so amazed, the cat
could talk, he gave him all these things.
The cat strode off into the woods
and hatched a plan to fool the King.
He caught some rabbits with the carrots,
and some pheasants with the grain.
He bagged them up to see the old King
in his Palace far away.

The road was long, the boots were hard,
and soon his feet began to ooze.
Green and putrid pools of pus
were filling up the leather boots!
When he reached the Palace hall
he sneaked into a nearby room.
He poured the pus into a bath,
then met the King that afternoon.

"Your Majesty", the cat proclaimed.
"I bring these gifts in gratitude.
from the Marquis of de Seet,
my Master, for his servitude."
The King was pleased to take the gifts,
and vowed to visit him next day.
The cat rushed home to tell the son
and passed some fields along the way.

He bribed the workers in the field
with pheasant, duck and rabbit meat,
to tell the King, the land belonged
to the Marquis of de Seet.
When morning came he took the son
back to the fields and said to him.
"Take off your old and ragged clothes,
and in the river take a swim."

The son did so, the cat then hid
the old clothes underneath a rock,
then rushed towards the Kings procession
shouting *"Help!"*, as if in shock
"Your Majesty, my Master drowns!
Some thugs have robbed him of his clothes!
They threw him in the River Ooze.
Save my Master from his woes!"

The servants dragged him out and gave
the son the finest clothes to wear.
The cat poured pus into the Ooze,
killing all the fish in there!
"Take my Master to his Castle,"
said the cat, *"It's to the west."*
The cat then ran ahead at speed
to carry out his final quest.

In this Castle lived an Ogre,
no one dared to venture close.
The cat crept in and saw a pot
of boiling pea soup on a stove.
The cat poured in more putrid pus,
then watched the Ogre slurp it down.
Soon there was a mighty crash;
The poisoned Ogre hit the ground!

The Kings' procession passed the workers
harvesting the fields of wheat.
They told him that the lands belonged
to this Marquis of de Seet.
The King dropped off the son and said;
*"I'm so impressed that you shall wed
My youngest daughter, just as soon
as she's recovered from her bed."*

*"She caught a really nasty rash
from a hot bath yesterday!"*
The daughter's beauty was well known.
The son agreed without delay.
The Marquis and the daughter wed.
A life of luxury they shared.
In the castle of the Ogre,
which they lovingly repaired.

The cat took off the leather boots
and never wore the things again.
He hung them on the Castle wall,
the boots that bought them wealth and fame!

The Three Lordly Pigs

*Based on **The Three Little Pigs**, an English fable first published in 1853.*

Once there lived a Farmer's daughter,
prim and proper, well refined.
One day three piglets they were born,
but sadly their poor mother died.
The daughter nurtured them for weeks,
and raised them fondly on her own.
The pigs enjoyed a charmed young life,
living in the Farmer's home.

The daughter told them it was time,
when all three pigs were fully grown.
To go into the **Pig**-wide world
and build themselves a starter home!
She told them they were wiser than
the other stupid farmyard pigs.
And they could use resources from
the farm to build their **Sty**-lish digs.

The first pig Haydon built his house
from several bays of hay and straw.
It had a **Pig**-turesque thatched roof
and charming woven wicker door.
The next pig Logan made a cabin
from old logs and lumber wood.
Surrounded by a **Pig-**ket fence,
he thought his house looked rather good!

The last pig built the grandest house.
His name was Rocco and he used
rocks and stones to build a fort.
The other pigs looked on bemused!
"Aren't you being a TRUFFLE cautious?"
said the first two pigs to him.
"With your feeble homes", said Rocco,
"You are risking life and limb!"

For a while they lived like Lords,
a life of leisure all day long.
Eating roast beef from the market,
what could possibly go wrong?
Rocco's fears were proved well founded.
Big bad Mr Wolf arrived.
Wiley, cunning, very hungry.
Three rich-**Pig**-king meals he spied!

He sneaked off to the nearby farmyard,
searching in some disused barns.
He then returned a short while later,
carrying items in his arms.
At the first house built of hay,
Mr Wolf cried *"Let me in!*
or else I'll use this box of matches
and this can of paraffin!"

"Oops", said Haydon, *"That was stupid;*
Should have built a fire-proof home.
Wish I'd been a bit less RASHER;
Pompous fool, I should have known!"
Haydon ran to Logan's lodge.
The wolf he followed taking time.
He banged upon its wooden door
and cried out *"Open up you SWINE!*

Or else I'll use this monster chainsaw
and huge axe upon your walls."
"Oops", said Haydon, *"Whoops"*, said Logan
"We have been conceited fools!"
Out the back the two pigs ran
and sheltered safe in Rocco's fort.
Mr Wolf strolled after them.
This plan was easier than he'd thought!

He banged on Rocco's great stone door;
Inside he heard a muffled clamour.
"Let me in, or else I'll use, this
PIG-axe and this large Sledge HAM-mer."
"Game on!" yelled the pigs inside
"Gammon", thought the Wolf instead.
They were getting on his nerves.
"I'm coming in!" the bored Wolf said.

"Ha ha ha!" replied faint Rocco.
"Not by the hair of your ugly chin!"
Mr Wolf he swung the **ham**mer
trying to smash the doorway in.
The **ham**mer made a tiny crack,
this fort was quite impregnable!
Mr Wolf would have to find
a way in more accessible.

The pigs inside, then heard faint **scratchings**
coming from the chimney stack.
But Rocco he had planned ahead
and used his next line of attack.
He had a pot of boiling oil,
placed underneath the chimney breast.
When the Wolf would hurtle down
he'd meet a painful gruesome death!

However Mr Wolf was smarter.
He had carried on his back
a barrel full of icy water
which he emptied down the stack!
The water hit the oil and filled
the room with hot and stinging steam.
Mr Wolf climbed down the chimney,
followed by three deathly screams!

Mr Wolf sat in his fortress.
Three fat pigs upon the spit.
He could finally relax
and put his paws up for a bit.
Haydon's hay was in abundance
for his spacious comfy bed.
Logan's logs fuelled his wood burner:
Life was good it could be said.

Suddenly within the doorway
standing there with a shotgun.
Screamed the Farmers' distraught daughter.
"You have killed them, every one!"
Mr Wolf he pulled a switch.
A trapdoor dropped her down a shaft!
Rocco was a clever builder;
He would eat that smart pig last!

Aladdin and the Tragic Lump

*Based on **Aladdin and the Magic Lamp**, a Middle Eastern folk lore tale first published in 1710.*

In a distant Persian village
lived a young apprentice lad.
Called Aladdin, he was always
getting into all things bad.
One day a greedy Sorcerer
persuaded him to bring him back
an oil lamp from a magic cave
full of deadly booby traps!

The Sorcerer sat in his robes
cooking morsels for his pets.
He munched on Cajun chicken breast,
on **OPEN SESAME** baguettes.
"All I need is an old lamp;
The other treasures can be yours."
And so Aladdin crept inside,
a wondrous sight filled him with awe!

The rusty lamp lay on a mound
of glistening precious gems and gold!
He rushed towards the treasure pile
forgetting what he had been told.
He stepped upon a booby trap
beneath a stone plate on the floor!
A giant boulder rolled behind him,
blocking off the cavern door!

He rushed ahead but stumbled over
hidden trip wires all around.
Poison arrows whizzed above him
as he fell towards the ground.
He crashed into the treasure mound,
the oil lamp toppled, then it fell.
The last thing he remembered was
it crashing hard upon his skull!

When he woke he heard a faint voice
coming from the cavern door.
*"Pass the lamp; there is a small gap
on your right side by the floor."*
Aladdin passed the oil lamp to
the eager Sorcerer outside.
He waited, then, *"It doesn't work
you useless boy!"* the Sorcerer cried.

The Sorcerer stormed off in rage.
Aladdin dropped down in despair.
His head was really throbbing now.
A large lump sprouted through his hair.
He rubbed the lump; there was a crackle,
then a blue explosive flash!
*"I am the Genie of the Lump,
three magic wishes you shall have!"*

Aladdin, he thought long and hard,
then rubbed his swollen lump again.
*"I wish to travel to my mum's house
with the treasure in this cave!"*
In an instance he was home.
Its walls were bursting at the seams!
Gold and gems were everywhere,
and he was rich beyond his dreams!

However, there was one downside;
His lump had doubled in its size!
Blue and bulbous, huge and ugly,
people stared in shocked surprise.
Several busy months passed by;
Aladdin moved into a Palace.
Then he asked the Village Sultan
for his daughter's hand in marriage.

The daughter eyed his ugly lump
but couldn't bring herself to wed.
And so he used his second wish
and rubbed the lump upon his head.
*"I wish that she would madly fall
in love with me despite my looks."*
Then instantly she changed her mind,
and soon the wedding day was booked!

Several blissful months passed by
until one tragic fateful night.
Aladdin he lay fast asleep,
his new wife felt a doubt inside.
She loved him dearly but felt saddened
for his bleak predicament.
Was he truly happy living
with his gross disfigurement?
She lovingly caressed the lump
and whispered softly in his ear.
*"You really are an ugly sight;
I wish that you would disappear!"*
Aladdin vanished in a puff!
"No!", she screamed, *"What have I done?"*
She cried for many days and nights,
distraught, regretful, overcome.

And then she realised she was pregnant
with Aladdin's unborn child.
At least a part of her Aladdin
would remain within this world.
She gave birth to a baby boy,
a perfect handsome child, except,
Aladdin Junior had a large blue,
lamp-shaped birthmark on his head!

Punoakio

*Based on **The Adventures of Pinocchio**, an Italian novel first published in 1883.*

In a town in Italy
lived Gelato old and grey.
A poor and lonely wood carver,
making wooden toys all day.
He made a boy from pine and oak,
a puppet called Pinoakio.
Gelato wished the boy were real,
a son that would mature and grow.

Suddenly it came to life!
A little wooden breathing boy!
Gelato danced with happiness,
so overcome with pride and joy.
He taught Pinoakio to read,
but one book gave the boy such fun.
Written by a Dominic Ricket;
The Bumper Book of Jokes and Puns!

He memorised this giant book
and soon was spouting puns galore.
Gelato put the boy on stage,
and soon his act would fill the floor.
But watching in the laughing crowd
a mother and her greedy son,
planned to steal Pinoakio
and tour the country with his puns.

And so that night they stole the boy
and locked him in a wooden cage.
And every night they rolled their star,
The **GREAT PUNOAKIO** on stage!
One night he faced an eager crowd,
the audience was really packed.
There was a hushed expectancy
as the boy began his act.

"About a month before he died
my Uncle he felt quite downcast.
He smeared some lard upon his back,
but after that went downhill fast!"

"Mr. Future, Past and Present
walked into a Country Inn.
The owner had to throw them out.
Things had got too tense for him!"

"My Boss said that he's going to fire
one of his new employees.
The one whose posture is the worst.
I have a hunch it might be me!"

"I threw a ball for my pet dog.
The whole thing cost a pretty packet.
But it was for his birthday and
he looks great in a dinner jacket!"

"I'll tell you what I love to do
more than anything itself.
Is squeezing into a small chest;
I hardly can contain myself!"

"To be run over by a steam train
was my friend's dream, quite absurd!
And when it finally happened he
was totally chuffed to bits, I've heard."

"I was told to stop pretending
being a Flamingo, by a friend.
Who was he to tell me that?
I put my foot down in the end!"

The audience they laughed and groaned.
"Release him from the cage!" they cried.
And so the mother and her son
reluctantly let out the child.
The audience rushed on the stage,
but when the crowd eventually cleared,
the mother and her son looked shocked.
Punoakio had disappeared!

Gelato, he'd been in the crowd
and now his treasured son was free.
He took him home to meet new siblings;
Willow, Ash and Ebony!

Mack and the Bairn Stork

*Based on **Jack and the Beanstalk**, an English fairy tale first published in 1734.*

In a Scottish Highland town
lived a mother with her son.
MacKinnon was the wee boys' name,
and known as Mack by everyone.
Life was hard, the townsfolk poor,
because a Giant from the Hills
would frequently ransack the town;
Their cattle sheep and pigs he'd steal.

One fine day, Macks' mother Morag
ordered him to sell their cow.
Maisie stopped producing milk
and was of little use right now.
And so Mack went to Loch Enlode
to sell poor Maisie at the Market,
where a strange Elf on the roadside
picked out Mack to be his target.

"I've three coloured magic beans;
They're great for farmers like yourself."
"I can't afford them." Mack replied.
"That's not a problem", said the Elf.
"I'll swap them for your scraggy cow!"
So Mack agreed and home did run.
Excited at the deal he'd made;
He'd have the proudest grateful mum!

"You stupid idiotic boy!
Off to your room!" his mother said.
And so Mack cried himself to sleep,
too mortified to leave his bed.
He woke to a loud knocking sound
upon his window, from outside.
He opened it to see a large Stork
carrying a baby child.

"I'm the Bairn Stork", said the bird.
"I have a small delivery.
It is a wee young baby boy
for the clan McCavity."
"Oh, that's the Dentists house," said Mack.
"But come back when you've finished please.
I have some coloured magic beans;
I'd really like your expertise."

The Stork returned to scan the beans.
"These beans are magical indeed!
The green bean is the Nature bean,
it brings amazing growing speed.
The blue bean is the Water bean,
producing huge freshwater lakes.
The red bean is the bean of Joy,
no more sorrow or heartaches!"

Mack asked him where the Bairns come from
as his Mum would not explain!
"From the clouds above that mountain,
Old Bairn Nevis is its name.
The Giant, he lives half way up
on a bare plain way up high.
He keeps your livestock in a cage;
I've often seen him when I fly."

Mack suddenly perceived a plan
and asked the Stork to fly him now.
To the plain, to make a truce
between the Giant and his town.
The Stork agreed and dropped him off;
Piles of bones lay far and wide.
And then as he crept near a hut
he heard a booming voice that cried.

"From Forfar to the Firth of Forth.
I smell the blood of Scottish birth.
Be he alive, or be he dead.
I'll grind his bones to fill my bread!"

Mack shouted, *"I am just a boy!*
I'm here to make a truce with you!
I've magic beans to bring you endless
happiness and boundless food!"
The Giant looked at little Mack.
A big Mack burger he'd prefer!
But as he felt quite curious,
this meagre meal he would defer.

Mack moved the livestock to the plain,
planting up the Nature Bean.
The livestock trebled in its size!
A meadow sprang up lush and green!
Mack then sowed the Water Bean
and several lakes appeared with fish!
The Giant ate the Bean of Joy
and made a heartfelt simple wish.

And soon a lonely Giantess
joined the Giant on the plain.
"Thank you boy", the Giant said,
"I'll never raid your town again."
Mack stayed a while and helped the Giant
build a homestead and a barn.
They'd be totally self-sufficient
in the way they ran their farm.

Mack then left them in his quest
to find the Bairns up in the clouds.
But sadly Mack did not return.
His statue in the town stands proud.

On a plaque beneath the statue
there's a message you will find:

"One small brave step for our Mack;
One Giant peace for all Clan Kind!"

THE END!

Vintage illustrations by Arthur Rackham, 1867-1939, taken from the Public Domain.

About the Author:

Steve Brown Lives in South Wales and hopes to live happily ever after, now that he has retired!
He enjoys writing poems and short stories, both serious and quirky.

Other books by the same Author:

Alternative Nursery Rhymes for Grown-ups.

Printed in Great Britain
by Amazon